The Evening Side of Morning

The Pre-Dawn Adventures of Dr. Maddog, Deaf Hugh, and Running Ralph

Mark D. Donnelly, PhD.

RPSS - Rock Paper Safety Scissors Publishing

RPSS - Rock, Paper, Safety Scissors Publishing
429 Englewood Avenue, Kenmore, NY 14223
publisher@rockpapersafetyscissors.com

978-1-956688-35-1 The Evening Side of Morning- Paperback

Printed in the USA

RPSS - ROCK PAPER SAFETY SCISSORS PUBLISHING

Recommended for fierce dreamers and hopeless insomniacs

Good morning.

My name is Dr. Maddog.

No one of any real importance actually calls me by that name. Still, it has been my email address since the invention of the Interweb.

It was a silly college nickname that I hoped would stick, but no such luck.

Goose the Cook
GET
SHIT
DONE

Dr. Maddog is now just the pen name and the avatar I use for the cookbooks I write.

It's a little awkward writing both children's books and cookbooks like Fifty Shades of Gravy under the same name.

Also, by hiding behind this canine persona, people will blame the dog if any of the recipes should ever go south.

It's zero dark thirty, with the emphasis on dark. It will be a couple of hours before the clouds replace the stars and the tsunami of endless phone, text, and email interruptions begins.

It's not that many centuries ago that this is the same time I would be rolling into the house after a night of frivolity.

It was plenty of time to change my shirt, brush the teeth that show, and head to work.

Now that I'm grayer, and the same age as old people, it's when I get up every day.

Waking up this early is an annoying habit.

They, whoever they are, say the early bird gets the worm. Rising before the birds and the worms have had a chance to hit the snooze button is my quiet time for reflection, imagination, and pathologic creativity.

I, unfortunately, sleep like a baby, up every couple of hours with a critical need to pee.

This schedule is part of my "what the heck" productivity plan. Since I'm already up, I might as well do some work.

Today is sure to be like any day because they're all pretty much the same.

My family claims it's my birthday, but that's impossible because I swear I just had one last week.

CNN

Every morning starts with the vague silhouette of me sitting at the edge of my chair, lit only by the glow of my CNN nightlight.

There's always a long windup before standing up because you can't rush into these things.

I do a mandatory morning preflight check to ensure all my human parts are functional enough to go vertical.

After waiting for gravity to take hold, I begin my zombie walk to the kitchen.

I can only describe the room as pitch black until they invent a darker color.

Daisy, part cat, and part furry assassin provides the daily obstacle course.

When she's not trying to suffocate me by sleeping on my face, she darts between my legs with each step toward the kitchen/bathroom to test my agility.

The only reason I tolerate this is because when calculated in cat- years, we're both about the same age.

If I somehow survive the cat challenge, it's time for the second part of the test- the kitchen lights.

Over a lifetime, I've been able to rid myself of most anxiety, with the possible exception of the kitchen light switch.

It's a dual switch tucked in an extremely awkward place, wedged between the coffee maker and refrigerator.

One switch turns on the light, and the other activates the noisiest garbage disposal ever made.

One is to break the darkness, and the other makes a blood-curdling banshee scream loud enough to wake the neighbors several houses down.

In the pre-coffee fog of the morning, choosing the correct switch is always a dicey gamble. Occasionally I get it right and the rest of the house can earn an extra hour or two of sleep.

I would hope no one believes I'm naturally this intense. Coffee is my rescue from sleep.

As a lifelong, card-carrying caffeine junkie, coffee rules my day.

I'm always hoping for a drum roll or a few bars of "Fanfare for the Common Man" when it's time for the start of the morning coffee ritual: the sacrificial grinding of the beans, the filling of the water, and the all-important selection of the day's mug.

Picking the wrong mug can really mess up your day. Choose wisely - the fate of humanity may depend on it.

This morning time used to be a lonely period of meditation, deep reflection, and dreaming with my eyes open.

That was until I discovered my 4 am breakfast club.

They're a bit non-traditional, but they've become my chosen morning family.

There's my friend Running Ralph.

The turning on of the coffee maker is his alarm clock. It's his queue to jump into action, instantly going from zero-to-sixty as he sprints a lap or two around the coffee pot and then the length of the countertop a few times before returning to his room to rest.

For a tiny yellow spider, this dude can make all those little legs really move.

He claims sleeping beside the caffeine delivery system has nothing to do with his extraordinary speed.

Ralph has hundreds of siblings and claims they're all just as handsome as he is.

He spends his daylight hours stalking and eating microscopic bugs that live on the window sill over the sink.

Now that I'm growing miniature pots of herbs like parsley, basil, and rosemary there, he says the kitchen deserves a 3-star Michelin rating.

He's promised me some recipes for my next cookbook.

My coffee maker's moan, groan, rattle, and purr are welcome songs that pierce the morning silence.

The guttural sounds are soon replaced by a beautiful fountain of burnt bean nectar, obviously invented by angels.

Ecstasy is near.

At coffee shops, the snotty
Barista's joke that I have a little
coffee with my cream.

I prefer to think of it as slightly
darkening my milk.

It's not a culinary choice - I'm old
and have a wussy stomach.

I now limit myself to precisely one
teaspoon of sugar - just enough to
settle on the bottom of a cup and
need a little physical intervention.

My first cup is solely to prime
the pump and build my strength
to have a second.

The next cup pumps the sunshine
into my smile, and the third and
fourth are to sharpen my
trademark passive-aggressive
snark.

For the sake of civil conversation,
my friends say I should always
stop at cup number two.

Enter the other member of my pre-dawn cohort – Deaf Hugh, or D.H., as his friends call him.

Hugh is an extraordinary old soul with a storied past.

More than a mere coffee stirrer, he was once the face of the famed Playboy Club.

HENCKELS

D.H. now lives in a wooden block that houses a family of German knives, all named Henckel.

He shares a slot with a 10-inch chef's knife that doesn't speak a syllable of English.

Fortunately, the Henckels are all great listeners. They haven't a clue what D.H. is endlessly bragging about, but they somehow appreciate the joy in his voice and the twinkle in his plastic eye while he talks.

In his youth, D.H.'s dynamic black silhouette became the logo of a chain of international nightclubs and resorts owned by his namesake, Hugh Hefner. His first job was at the Playboy Club when it opened in Chicago in 1960.

For many years, Hugh sat on the piano of Sam Distefano. Sam would use Hugh like a conductor's baton when he led the 32-piece house orchestra.

Hugh was skillfully waved for performers such as Dean Martin, Sammy Davis Jr., Tony Bennett, Wayne Newton, and dozens of other superstars whose names will only impress you if you're really old.

Hugh loves to tell the story about the night a close-up magician who worked the Club Room made him disappear, only to suddenly reappear firmly wedged in a Playboy Bunnies cleavage.

His memories of the waitress who would eventually become Playboy magazine's Miss July are crystal clear.

In fact, they get clearer and more detailed each and every time he tells the story.

In 1991, the Playboy Club chain became defunct, and the next few years became a blur of thrift stores and silverware drawers.

Hugh eventually surfaced in a basement bar in the home of Chet and Terry, an old Polish couple whose last name he could never pronounce or spell.

They lived in a middle class suburb of Buffalo, New York.

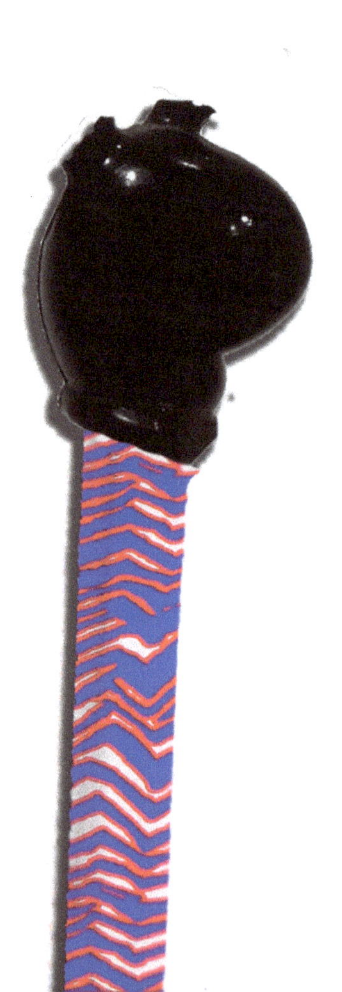

To fit in, Hugh quickly changed his loyalties from supporting Da Bears to a table-crushing, condiment-squirting Buffalo Bills fan.

The pine-paneled bar he now worked was ground zero for many weekends of socially lubricating family and friends.

It wasn't the glitz and celebrity of Chicago, but these were happy times, and it was good to be employed again.

With the sad passing of Chet in 2015, the bar and all the assorted bar hardware, like Hugh, were packed up by his daughter, Princess Laura.

It was then taken to our house because you can never have enough stuff.

Fortunately, this is far from the end of this story. Even though Princess Laura and I are not drinkers, Hugh was repurposed from cocktail swizzle stick to a professional coffee stirrer.

Now scuffed up and missing both his ears, broken off during all the transporting around, he's thrilled to be working and a vital part of the family.

D.H. brings some exceptional skill sets to his new profession. Because he is ambidextrous, he can stir coffee both clockwise and counterclockwise.

Although unable to hear and without hands to sign, Hugh has become a fantastic lip reader.

Being old-school and proud to be thoroughly politically incorrect, he prefers the term deaf over hearing impaired or hearing challenged.

He likes to brag that even without ears, he can hear better than most other coffee stirrers. It comes from his years of working behind a bar.

Being an attentive and sympathetic listener really adds to the tip jar.

Working for teetotalers has admittedly been a challenge for D.H..

There's a world of difference between dodging ice cubes in a cocktails glass, and the near-boiling hot tub of a cup of coffee.

Fortunately for Hugh, because of his advancing age, the parts of him most sensitive to temperature are missing in action.

I often place some tiny cocktail umbrellas in my morning brew to try and ease his transition. He's not impressed, but I think it adds a little class to the joint.

I wet my plants!

Happy Water The Plants Day

When I say that all days are the same, there are, of course, exceptions.

Every Tuesday is:

"Happy Water The Plants Day."

One of my life's greatest disappointments is this weekly celebration I originated never caught on as a Hallmark card-level holiday.

I've even designed my own cards to try and jumpstart a populist movement.

STAY BACK
FEET

The other red-letter day is Friday morning.

I dramatically race to take out the trash each week before the garbage truck arrives.

It wouldn't be such a big deal if I took it out the night before like everyone else in the neighborhood.

This adrenaline surge adds a bit of extra spice to the end of each week.

MISSING

FULL NAME

Date of Birth:

Age:

Sex or gender:

Race:

Eyes:

Hair:

Height:

Weight:

Wearing:

Identifying Characteristics:

CLEAR PHOTO

LAST SEEN: MONTH, DAY, YEAR

IF YOU HAVE ANY INFORMATION ABOUT (NAME) PLEASE CONTACT:

While we may sound boring, this morning crew isn't without its occasional adventure.

A couple of times a year, Deaf Hugh goes missing because he is mistaken for something disposable or discarded because he's broken.

The 911 operator is no longer amused.

After a thorough manhunt, usually ending in dumpster diving, we are all reunited.

We celebrate with coffee, sporting tiny umbrellas.

About a month ago, my 94-year-old mother told me with great pride that she had just killed a spider in the kitchen, and she poured its lifeless remains down the sink.

I was devastated. Though tiny, Running Ralph had a supersized role in my pre-dawn circle.

His frenetic antics had been a great source of entertainment, and his resilience served as an important role model.

I spent most of that afternoon arranging a memorial service and preparing to hand out black armbands.

R.I.P.

BOB

At its usual appointed time the following day, I turned on the coffee machine.

To my delight, a very undead Ralph popped out, did his daily laps and sprints, and returned to his miniature home as though nothing had happened.

This whole adventure was, fortunately, just a matter of mistaken identity.

It was actually Bob, one of Ralph's hundreds of identical cousins that met this unseemly demise. We held a funeral in Bob's honor anyway.

May he rest in peace.

General Mills

CRISPY CRUNCHY
WHOLE WHEAT FLAKES

WHEATIES

THE BREAKFAST OF CHAMPIONS®

BILLS
17

Josh Allen

TOASTED 100% WHOLE
WHEAT FLAKES

My morning family is a band of fierce dreamers.

Running Ralph yearns to be on a Wheaties box and is looking for an agent in the hopes of securing a sneaker endorsement.

Ralph thinks Nike should use him as a replacement for Tiger Wood.

KitchenAid

When Deaf Hugh isn't reminiscing about his glory days at the Club, he secretly aspires to be in the hands of a famous Maestro conducting an Orchestra again.

When the house is at its quietest, I hear humming floating in from the kitchen.

It's either Hugh practicing classical music that he's committed to memory, or the refrigerator sounds like Beethoven.

The romantic in me hopes it's Hugh.

IZABETHA VXOR
ENRICI VII

As proof that coffee solves everything, our daily group discussion is the highlight of each morning. It's incredible how easily we can solve all the world's issues over a single cup of Joe.

The White Queen says she's believed as many as six impossible things before breakfast. She has an open invitation to join our group.

We discuss highbrow intellectual topics such as Middle East peace, corporate gains, Coke vs. Pepsi, Wordle streaks, and how cold it needs to be before wearing socks.

To facilitate a civil conversation, we each raise our hand to speak next. Ralph, by the nature of his multiple arms, tends to dominate the conversation completely.

By contrast, D.H., lacking arms altogether, always feels slighted, and consistently breaks this rule.

Daisy, the cat, occasionally tries to join in. She, unfortunately, knows only one word, said with multiple inflections.

Her topics only focus on eating, sleeping, and chasing the laser dot.

Before long, the dog next door begins barking, and there is the familiar thump on the porch of the daily newspaper.

A brief look out the window shows where the sky has been eating the darkness and coloring it with the whole box of Crayons (with sharpener).

This my old man version of Homer's "the child of morning, rosy- fingered dawn."

It's all part of his formula that things have an eternal, infinitely repeatable presence.

Different things will happen every day, but the dawn always appears, always with rosy fingers, and always early.

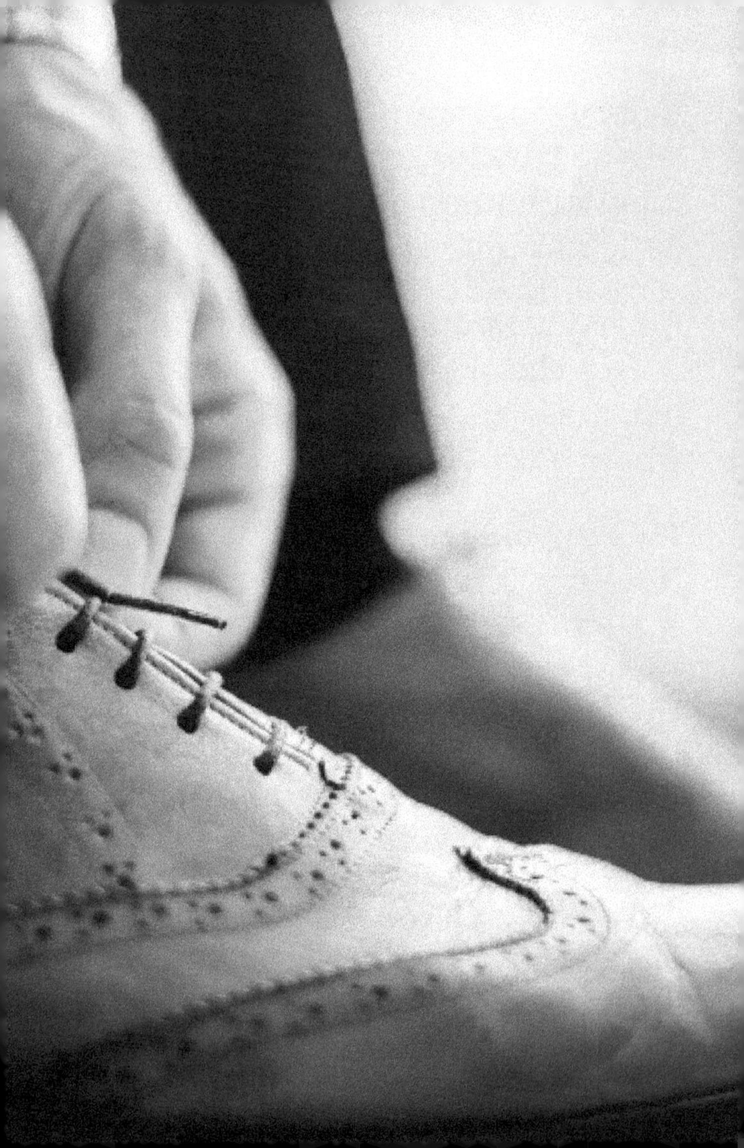

The bliss of quiet is beginning to break with the realization that it's nearing the moment for starched shirts, tight shoes, and the appearance of rational thought.

It's that time again to open my eyes the rest of the way and dive head first into the new day's journey with all the chaos and opportunity it will surely bring.

I can confidently muddle forward, knowing that the last threeish cups of coffee have put enough of a bounce in my step and a smile on my face. Zero dark thirty will arrive all too soon again.

Hopefully, tonight we can finally resolve the Coke versus Pepsi debate.

Postscript:

Although I will miss his stories and sheer perfection in how he stirs my coffee, I have agreed to place Deaf Hugh in an envelope and mail him to his idle, JoAnn Falletta, the Buffalo Philharmonic Orchestra's music director.

Deep down in my heart, I know they can make fantastic music together in her hands.

D.H. also wants you to know that he's still a stud.

General Mills
CRISPY CRUNCHY
WHOLE WHEAT FLAKES
WHEATIES®
THE BREAKFAST OF CHAMPIONS®
WHEATIES
BILLS
17
Josh Allen
TOASTED 100% WHOLE
WHEAT FLAKES
NET WT 15.6 OZ (442g)

Running Ralph has partially found success.

He is now on a Wheaties box.

Actually, he's in the pantry proudly standing on a Wheaties box.

He's found great joy there,
so please don't tell him the difference.

He's also still waiting for Nike to return his calls.

Miss July is now a mother of four and leads a happy life working as a cashier at the Dollar Store.

She has no recollection of D.H.'s story that she starred in.

Daisy sleeps most of the day,
dreaming up new ways to kill me.

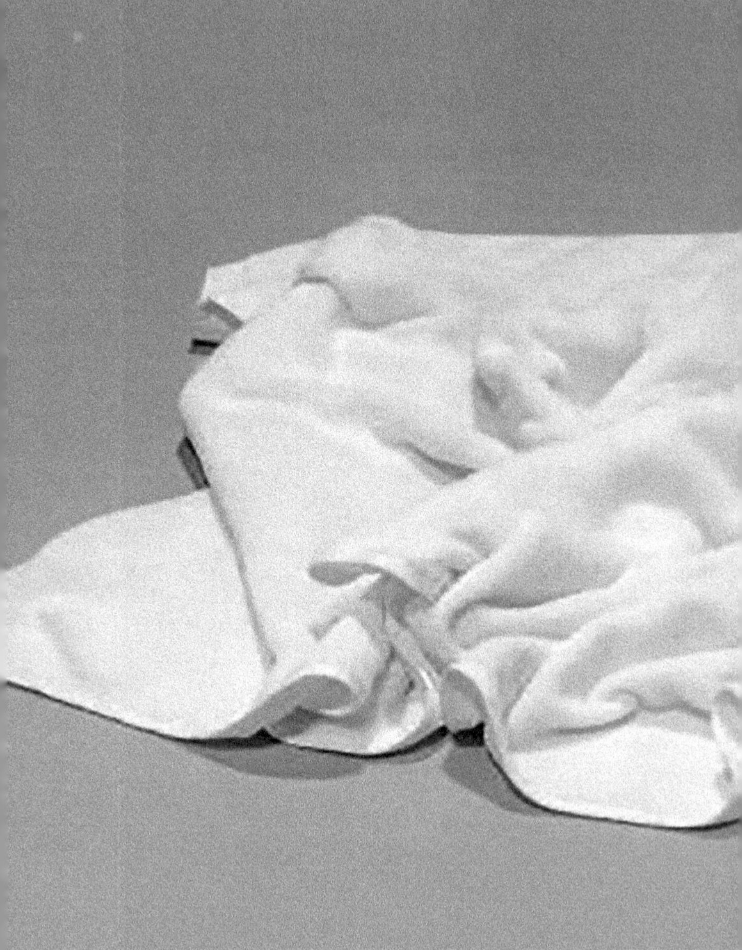

Princess Laura is still beautiful and continues to pick up my towels because she loves me.

My mother is currently serving 20-to-life with no hope of parole for the savage murder of Bob.

Oktoberfest

And on a curious note, a handful of the Henkel family left for Octoberfest.

The strange part is that it's only February.

My family has given up thinking that I've totally lost a grasp of reality.

They blew past that milestone ages ago.

I'm still the luckiest man ever.

-Dr. Maddog